My "w" Sound Box®

(The "wh" sound is included in this book.)

Library of Congress Cataloging-in-Publication Data
Moncure, Jane Belk.
My "w" sound box / by Jane Belk Moncure; illustrated by Colin King.
p. cm.
Summary: A little girl fills her sound box with many words beginning with the letter "w."
ISBN 1-56766-789-9 (lib. reinforced : alk. paper)
[1. Alphabet.] I. King, Colin, ill. II. Title.
PZ7.M739 Myw   2000
[E]—dc21   99-056564

My "w"
Sound Box®

Jane Belk Moncure

illustrated by Colin King

The Child's World®

Little  had a box.

"I will find things that begin
with my 'w' sound," she said.

"I will put them into my sound box."

Little **w** went for a walk in the woods. She found . . .

woodpeckers

and a woodchuck.

Did she put them into her box? She did.

Little  looked under some wood chips. She found lots of wiggly worms.

"In you go," she said.

Little walked to a well in the woods. She drank some water from the well.

"This may be a wishing well," she said. She looked all around the well.

Guess what she found? It was a wand.

Little waved her wand and made a wish.

"I wish I could find more things for my box," she said.

Just then,

a weasel  wiggled into the box
as quick as a wink.

A big wolf was after him!

Little  waved her wand.

"I wish you would be a good wolf," she said. She put the wolf into her box with the  weasel, the woodpecker, the wiggly worms, and the woodchuck.

Now the box was full.

Little  found a wheelbarrow.

"Whee," she said.
"This is just what I need." She wheeled the
wheelbarrow and away they went . . .

up and down a winding road to the water.

"Let's wade in the water," she said.

But the wolf, weasel, woodpecker, wiggly worms, and woodchuck did not want to wade. They watched.

"Wow," said a walrus.

"You look wacky to me.
You have funny feet."

"You look wacky to me," said Little

"You have funny whiskers."

Little  put the walrus into the box.

The walrus winked
at the wolf.

Little  went back to the water.

The wind blew the waves up and down.

Then she saw . . . .

a big whale. The whale whistled.

"I wish I could put the whale in my box, but it is too big," she said.

Little  waved her wand and found a big

wagon.

It was big enough for a whale.

She put all of her things into the wagon
and walked into . . .

a wall.

What was behind the wall?

"Whoopee," whooped the woodpecker when he saw the

watermelons.

"Let's have a watermelon party," said Little . And they did.

wolf

wheelbarrow

watermelons

wiggly worms

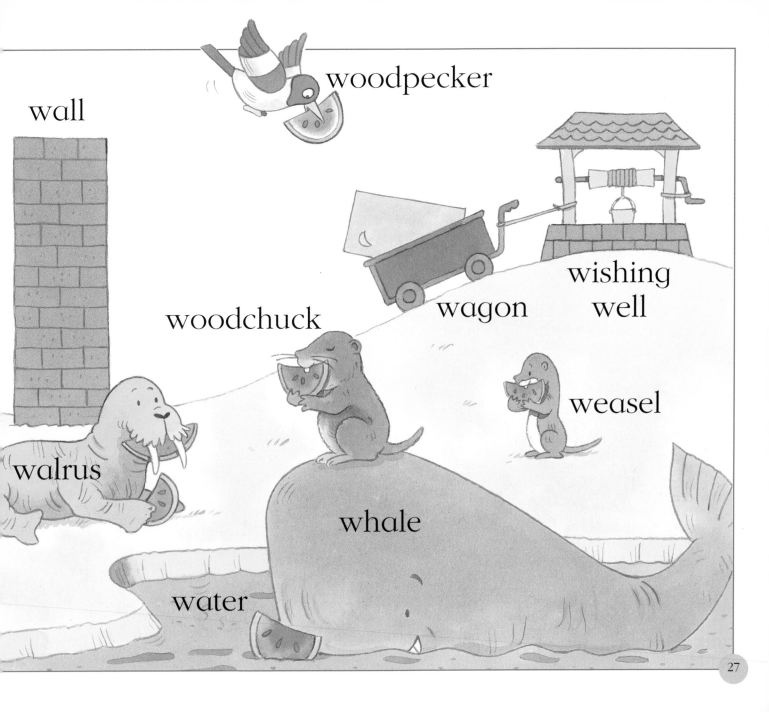

woodpecker

wall

woodchuck

wishing
well

wagon

weasel

walrus

whale

water

27

Can you read these words

with Little **w** ?

watch

window

woman

wallet

web

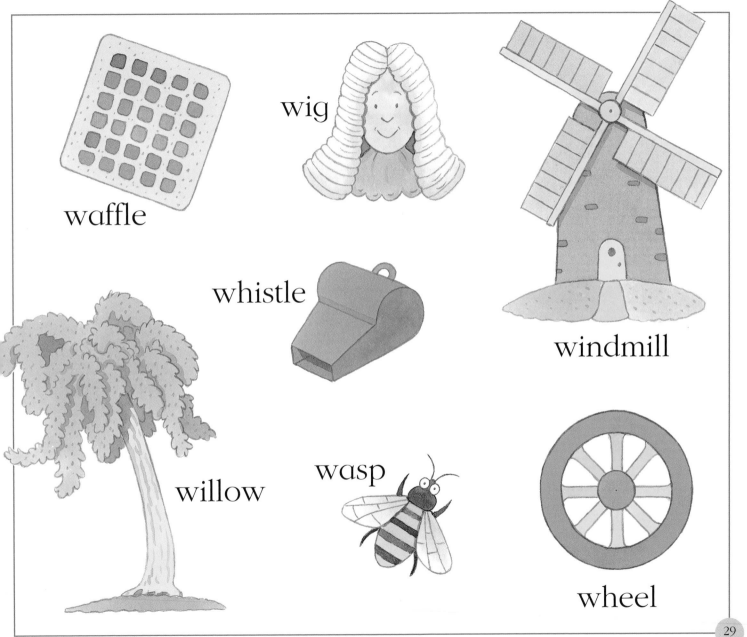

waffle

wig

windmill

whistle

willow

wasp

wheel

I WISH

ABOUT THE AUTHOR AND ILLUSTRATOR

Jane Belk Moncure began her writing career when she was in kindergarten. She has never stopped writing. Many of her children's stories and poems have been published, to the delight of young readers, including her son Jim, whose childhood experiences found their way into many of her books.

Mrs. Moncure's writing is based upon an active career in early childhood education.
A recipient of an M.A. degree from Columbia University, Mrs. Moncure has taught and directed nursery, kindergarten, and primary grade programs in California, New York, Virginia, and North Carolina. As a former member of the faculties of Virginia Commonwealth University and the University of Richmond, she taught prospective teachers in early childhood education.

Mrs. Moncure has travelled extensively abroad, studying early childhood programs in the United Kingdom, The Netherlands, and Switzerland. She was the first president of the Virginia Association for Early Childhood Education and received its award for outstanding service to young children.

A resident of North Carolina, Mrs. Moncure is currently a full-time writer and educational consultant. She is married to Dr. James A. Moncure, former vice president of Elon College.

Colin King studied at the Royal College of Art, London. He started his freelance career as an illustrator, working for magazines and advertising agencies.

He began drawing pictures for children's books in 1976 and has illustrated over sixty titles to date.

Included in a wide variety of subjects are a best-selling children's encyclopedia and books about spies and detectives.

His books have been translated into several languages, including Japanese and Hebrew. He has four grown-up children and lives in Suffolk, England, with his wife, three dogs, and a cat.